PHILADELPHIA

THIS BOOK
BELONGS TO:

‑‑‑‑‑‑‑‑‑‑‑‑‑‑‑‑‑‑‑‑

‑‑‑‑‑‑‑‑‑‑‑‑‑‑‑‑‑‑‑‑

CREATED & WRITTEN BY ROBIN BARONE
ILLUSTRATED BY DANIEL LEE

THIS BOOK IS DEDICATED TO

The travelers who went before me, alongside me, and those yet to come.

ABOUT WHERE IS ROBIN?

We are a platform that uses adventure travel to teach children about the world.

- DREAM - - PLAN - - GO -

For sales inquiries, contact sales@diplomatbooks.com.

DIPLOMAT BOOKS

Diplomat Books
New York, New York

www.diplomatbooks.com

www.whereisrobin.org

ISBN 978-0-9906310-5-7

MADE WITH ♥
IN THE USA

Robin boarded the SEPTA train and headed into Center City.
Looking out the window, she thought that the skyline was pretty!

At 30th Street Station, the train arrived.
Her city tour started outside.

In West Philadelphia, Robin sat on College Green.
This campus was the most exciting place she'd seen!

The University of Pennsylvania was founded by Benjamin Franklin.
Looking at Locust Walk Robin asked, "When do classes begin?"

West Philadelphia has America's first zoo.
It was built during the Civil War - who knew?

The zoo cares for wildlife far from their natural home.
Standing under the Big Cat Crossing, Robin watched a tiger roam.

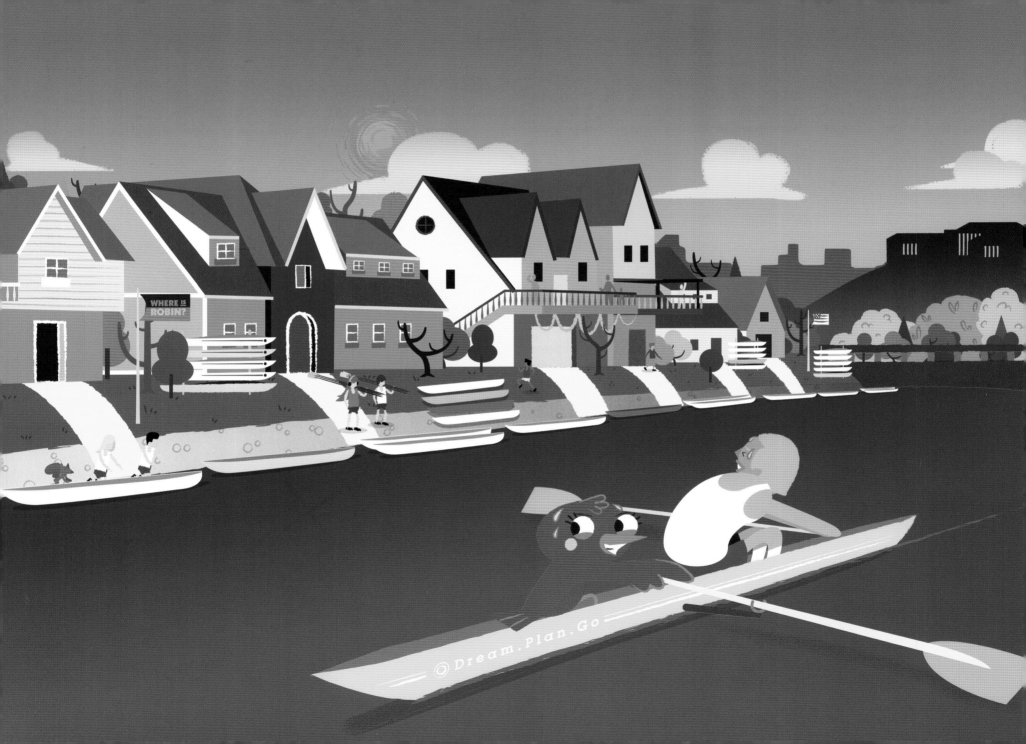

On the Schuylkill River's east bank is Kelly Drive.
It's where Boathouse Row keeps rowing traditions alive!

With her short legs, Robin rowed port in the bow.
"Robin, extend your wings further. Let me show you how!"

Robin ran up the steps of the Museum of Art and reached the entrance.
She admired Philadelphia, a city design inspired by France.

From atop the stairs, Robin looked at the flags along the parkway.
Flags from around the world were hung to celebrate Bicentennial Day.

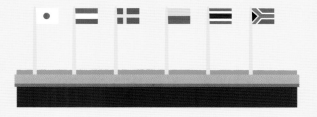

Robin explored the Philadelphia Museum of Art.
The latest exhibition stole her heart!

Art from around the world called the Museum home.
The collection inspired Robin's dreams to roam.

Along the Parkway, Robin discovered museums to experience culture. One of her favorite places was the Rodin Museum for sculpture.

Her favorite statue sat in front of the courtyard. To see it in person was better than a postcard!

Impressionist artists Renoir, Cezanne, Matisse, and more—
The largest collection of their art is found through the Barnes' doors!

Dedicated to art appreciation, the museum was founded by Dr. Barnes.
Too excited during her visit, Robin accidentally tripped one of the alarms!

Heading along the Parkway past Swann Fountain in the park, Robin walked up the stairs into a literary landmark.

The Free Library of Philadelphia promotes learning and literacy. It's the perfect place for Robin to nurture her curiosity.

At the Franklin Institute, Robin joined a tour about to start.
Her favorite exhibit of was walking through the human heart!

The Franklin Institute inspires a love of science and technology.
The Institute is a world dedicated to discovery!

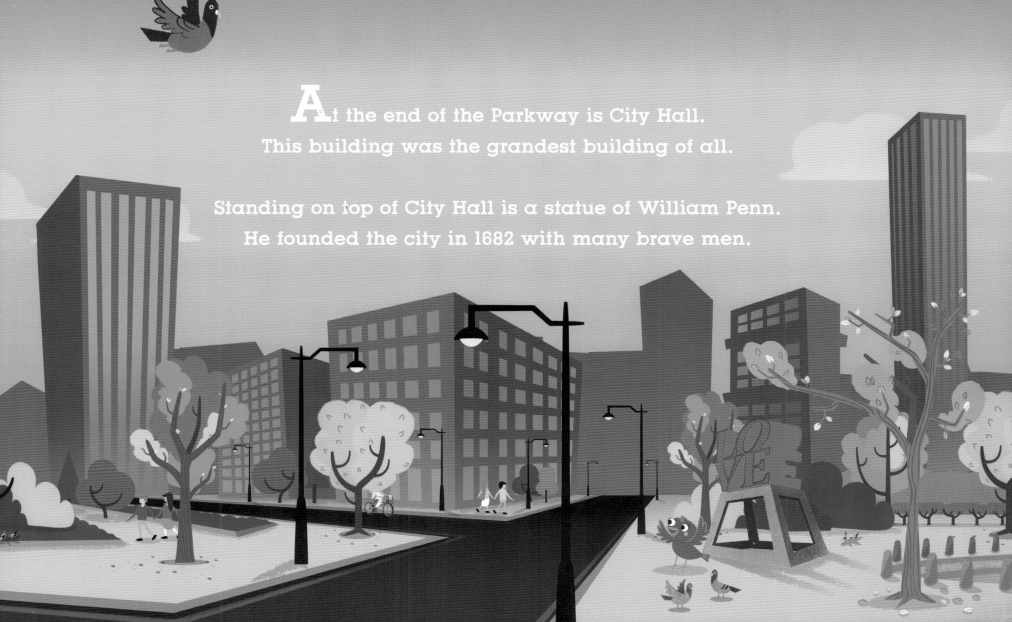

At the end of the Parkway is City Hall.
This building was the grandest building of all.

Standing on top of City Hall is a statue of William Penn.
He founded the city in 1682 with many brave men.

In the heart of Center City, Rittenhouse Square is the best.
By the lion statue was Robin's favorite spot to rest.

Rittenhouse Square is a park designed by William Penn.
It was named "Southwest Square" way back then.

At the Kimmel Center, Robin was invited to perform on stage.
Would the Orchestra offer her a seat at this young age?

The Kimmel Center is located on the Avenue of the Arts.
The Orchestra's performance captured the audience's hearts!

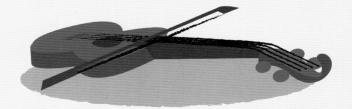

At Reading Terminal, Robin discovered the ultimate food market.
"There are so many choices. What should I get?"

Fresh from the farm of the Pennsylvania Dutch,
Robin ate an amazing lunch!

FREEDOM IS A LIGHT
FOR WHICH MANY MEN HAVE DIED IN DAR

Dream . Plan . Go

Washington Square is a great park!
It's home to the Tomb of the Unknown Soldier, a famous landmark.

Here, Robin learned about the American Revolution.
Our founding fathers thought independence was the best solution.

The United States was born at Independence Hall.
Our founding fathers dreamed of life with liberty for all.

Here, the Declaration of Independence and Constitution were signed.
These documents keep our country's values of freedom and liberty in mind.

The Liberty Bell was created for the tower at Independence Hall.
The inscription on the bell proclaims "Liberty for all."

The bell cracked when it was first rung.
Unfortunately, the bell could not be hung.

The laws of our country were written in the Constitution.
At the Constitution Center, Robin learned about this institution.

The Constitution created three branches for the government
and gave people the power to elect officials that represent.

Robin visited the home of Betsy Ross in Old City.
She was the most famous flag maker in American History.

The design was based on a legal resolution
that the stars and stripes represent every colony in the Union.

On a horse drawn carriage, Robin toured Society Hill.
She was far from where her trip began near the Schuylkill.

Along the cobblestone streets to Headhouse Square,
Robin loved touring this city in the open air!

Continuing east Robin reached the waterfront.
She boarded a boat for a cruise - what else could an adventurer want!

Along the Delaware River, Robin admired the skyline.
She loved how the building lights made it shine!

Heading south, Robin found a museum that celebrated mummery!
"A local tradition since 1901 for fun" was written in the museum's summary.

Dream . Plan . Go

Robin imagined walking down Broad Street in the New Year's Day Parade.
She was dressed in costume while the string bands played!

A visit to the sports stadium makes the day complete.
Local fans and their passion cannot be beat!

Robin imagined herself playing against the birds.
The birds against Robin - there are no words!

"**H**ey it's my Robin. Let's have dinner before you go!"
"Pops, the city is amazing! So much history that I didn't know!"

"There are so many places in this world to see!
Don't worry. I will always come home for my family!"

Join all of Robin's adventures!

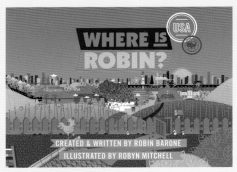

Where is Robin? USA
ISBN: 978-0-9906310-9-5

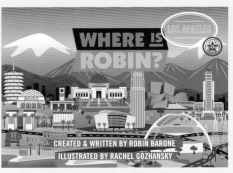

Where is Robin? Los Angeles
ISBN: 978-0-9906310-8-8

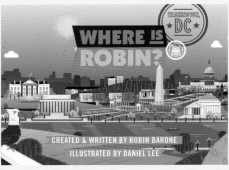

Where is Robin? Washington DC
ISBN: 978-0-9906310-6-4

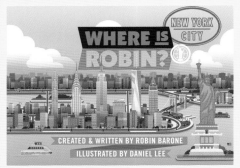

Where is Robin? New York City
ISBN: 978-0-9906310-4-0

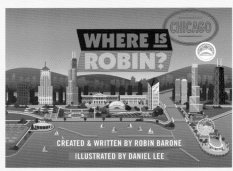

Where is Robin? Chicago
ISBN: 978-0-9906310-7-1

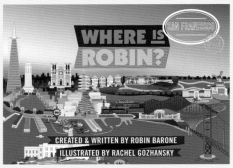

Where is Robin? San Francisco
ISBN: 978-1-9465640-6-1

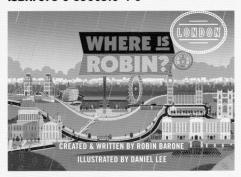

Where is Robin? London
ISBN: 978-1-9465642-6-9

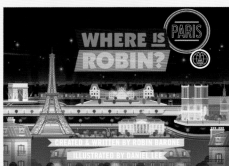

Where is Robin? Paris
ISBN: 978-1-9465642-7-6

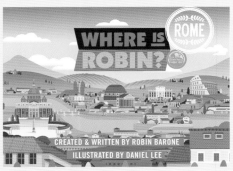

Where is Robin? Rome
ISBN: 978-1-9465642-8-3

Let's keep traveling together. Sign up for our newsletter at www.whereisrobin.org
and share pictures with us on social media by tagging #whereisrobinusa.